Marge in Charge

AND THE
MISSING ORANGUTAN

Also by Isla Fisher

Marge in Charge

Marge in Charge and the Stolen Treasure

Marge
in
Charge

AND THE
MISSING ORANGUTAN

ISLA FISHER

Illustrated by Eglantine Ceulemans

HARPER

An Imprint of HarperCollinsPublishers

ISBN 978-0-06-266224-8

19 20 21 22 23   CG/LSCH   10 9 8 7 6 5 4 3 2 1

First U.S. edition, 2019
Originally published in the U.K. by Picadilly Press
under the title *Marge and the Great Train Rescue*

For my grandmother Anna,
who taught me to love books,
and for Olive, Elula,
Monty, and Sacha
—I.F.

the Button Family

Mommy

Dad

Jake

Me
(Jemima)

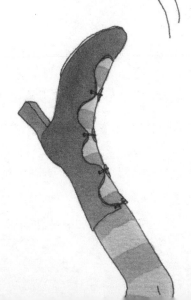

Marge and the Missing Tooth

"COME OUT!" I say.

My four-year-old brother is hiding under his bed.

"Marge is here!" I am so happy.

Marge, the best babysitter in the whole universe, is at our house, and my little brother doesn't care. I don't know what is wrong with him. Marge is not like a normal, boring babysitter. Marge is just the opposite: she is a member of the royal family, and she once helped us build a dinosaur out of pancakes.

Mommy and Dad appear in the doorway looking sharp. Dad is in a suit and Mommy is wearing a fancy black shirt.

"We have to leave for the party now. Please come out," Dad begs.

"NO!" Jakey sounds mad. This is not like him at all. Usually when he hears that Marge is coming, he pulls his shorts over his head like a wrestling mask and races to the door to greet her.

I walk with our parents to the hallway where Marge is waiting. I always forget how small she is. Even though I am only seven years old, I am nearly as tall as our grown-up babysitter. She can even fit inside our play tent without bending over.

Today she is wearing a shiny silver shirt and a strange silver hat.

"Greetings, earthling," Marge jokes, giving me a robotic wave. She does look a little like she has come from outer space, and I giggle.

"We won't be back until late." Dad gives me a hug. "And remember, Marge is in charge!"

"See if you can cheer Jakey up," Mommy says as she grabs her car keys. "He's been under that bed since he got home from school." Then, as she is half out the door, she remembers. "I left the rules on the fridge."

Usually Marge adds things to Mommy's rules to make them more fun, like the time when she took us to Theo's birthday party. Marge changed Mommy's rule about only eating one slice of cake at the party to *nine* slices!!

The minute we have waved off our old blue car, Marge does my favorite thing. She takes off her hat and shakes out her long rainbow hair. It is so crazy—red, green, yellow, orange, and blue.

"Let's go cheer up your brother!" Marge dances down the corridor and into our bedroom. I am getting very mad at Jakey; it's so exciting to have Marge here, and all he is doing is hiding and ruining the fun.

I want Marge to tell us wild stories about
when she lived in the palace or traveled the
world with her fourteen pets.

"Jakey?" Marge pretends she can't see his
legs poking out from underneath the bed.

"Yoo-hoo," she calls, checking behind the
curtains and inside my closet.

"Where are youuuuuu?" she sings.

"I'm under here," a little voice replies.

Marge hoists up her skirt and crawls under his bed. I wriggle in after her until we are both facing Jakey.

My brother's face is blotchy and red.

"Whatever is the matter?" Marge asks. "I haven't seen such a sad face since the marquis of Humperdink played tennis in the ballroom and smashed his favorite Ming vase."

"My tooth won't come out." Jakey's bottom lip is quivering. "I've had this stupid wobbly tooth for so long and it won't budge!"

"That is terrible news." Marge looks grave.

"Theo lost a tooth and the tooth fairy gave him a whole quarter!" Theo has one long eyebrow and is Jakey's best friend from school.

"The tooth fairy is never going to visit me," Jakey whimpers.

"Never say never, Jakeypants," Marge tells him. "I remember when I thought I was never going to see my hairy-nosed wombat, George, again after he buried himself underneath the castle moat, but then, one day, there he was! Sunning himself on the queen's lounge chair, drinking tea and wearing her missing tiara."

Marge shuffles closer to Jakey. "Can I see?" She gently wobbles his tooth with her finger.

"I've tried pulling it out," Jakey says, sniffling. "I've wiggled and pushed, but it's stuck."

"Dentist Marge to the rescue!" Marge exclaims, and at last Jakey smiles. "All we need is your dad's toolbox."

The smile runs away from my little brother's face, and he looks a little frightened as we all crawl backward out from under the bed.

Then Marge tells me that I will be the dental assistant, which I am actually quite excited about.

"I once removed my Persian cat Amelia's left fang, after she broke into the palace pantry and ate too many candies. It was rotten to the core!" Marge tells Jakey. "I also pulled a tooth that had been stuck in a suit of armor in the castle for a thousand years. The knight didn't feel a thing!"

I run to the garage and come back with Dad's toolbox and Marge whistles as she searches through it. I have the brilliant idea that we might need protective gear in case there is blood, so I grab an apron from the kitchen.

"Lie down," I tell Jakey as Marge puts on a gigantic pair of goggles.

"Open up! WIDE."

Marge and I peer at Jakey's teeth. They are white and pearly, and even though Mommy always says that he doesn't brush his teeth for long enough, they do look quite sparkly.

The toolbox is red and shiny, and it has lots of weird and wonderful things inside it.

"Too big. . . ." Marge shakes her head as she pulls out a wrench.

"Too heavy...." Marge puts the hammer back.

"Too screwy...." She dismisses the screwdriver.

"Voilà!" She grins, waving a pair of green pliers.

"Perfect!"

In case you don't know, pliers are like metal claws used for gripping things.

I am not sure exactly what Marge is going to do with the pliers, as I have only seen Dad use them to pull nails out of the fence, but I am just the dental assistant, not the dentist. I'm also a little worried that our parents might not be very happy if they could see us now, but it was Mommy who told us to cheer up Jakey, and he is definitely being cheered up, because even though he is scared, Jakey loves having people fuss over him.

"Maybe you should close your eyes," I suggest, and he shuts them tight.

"Eeny, meeny, miny, mo,
This little tooth has got to go!"

Marge sings as she leans over Jakey. She

grasps the loose tooth with the pliers and braces her leg against the side of the bed.

"ARGHHHHH!"

Marge has fallen backward and landed with her feet in the air, but the tooth is still *inside* Jakey's mouth.

"The tooth is too wet for the pliers to grip," I say, deciding that I am really good at being a dental assistant.

"No, it must be superglued in!" Jakey sits up.

Then I have the most obvious idea. I can't believe that I haven't thought of it before. Jakey just needs to eat an apple! That's how I lost my tooth. But then I remember my little brother has two rules:

1. He will only eat his dinner if there is a pool of tomato ketchup in the center of his plate that his veggies can "swim" in.

2. He hates apples. He won't eat an apple since the day he found out that worms can live in them.

"I know you hate them, but you have to eat an apple to make your tooth come out," I tell Jakey, and to my surprise he bolts into the kitchen.

Marge and I share a look as Jakey holds out a big green apple and then takes an enormous bite.

CHOMP!

He chews a bit and swallows.

"It's still the same amount of wobbly." Jakey sighs. "And this apple definitely tastes like worm poop."

After that we tie a piece of string around Jakey's tooth and onto Archie's collar (Archie is our pug-nosed puppy dog) and try to get him to go for a run, but he won't and we are close to giving up when . . .

"I've got it!" I point to Jakey's remote-controlled monster truck parked in the kitchen doorway.

Jakey and Marge look at it too. Silently we nod our heads in agreement.

I tie the string around Jakey's tooth, and Marge fastens the other end to the back of the truck.

Jakey has the remote. He looks determined as he pushes the control to Forward.

The truck takes off, shooting across the floor and the string grows taut. . . .

POP!

Jakey's tooth flies out of his mouth. It's still attached to the string.

FINALLY!

Jakey grabs his tooth, and we all race to the hallway. In the mirror I can see that there is a big hole where Jakey's wobbly tooth used to be! Jakey whoops with joy. I really am a great dental assistant.

"I remember when my long-toothed ferret Burt lost his first tooth," Marge says proudly. "We put it at the end of his bed— it was too long to fit under his pillow—and the tooth fairy brought him five hundred dollars. Long-toothed ferrets' teeth are extremely valuable."

"The tooth fairy will be in our room tonight." I am jumping up and down. This is almost as exciting as the times she visited *me*. Jakey gives Marge a big hug. I told you Marge is the best babysitter in the whole world.

"All right, let's read your mommy's

instructions." Marge claps her hands. "Hop to it!"

So we all take a careful look at the list of rules Mommy has left for us:

1. Dinner at 6:30 p.m.

2. Bath time — no need to wash hair

3. Brush teeth before bed!

4. Lights out at 8 p.m.

Marge checks her watch. "It's six p.m. now, so we have plenty of time before lights-out."

I am so happy Marge is here and Jakey-pants is no longer Grumpypants! My little brother names his tooth Tim, and Tim the Tooth takes part in all our games and even comes to dinner. It's so much fun having a tooth to play with. Tim can ride in tiny cars, he can fly to the moon in our Lego rocket, he can sleep in a matchbox, and he can even be a pretend pearl in our underwater diving game. In between activities Marge reminds Jakey to wrap Tim the Tooth in a little bit of tissue and keep him safely inside his pocket, but after our bath Jakey feels in there for Tim and screams.

"ARGGHHHH!"

"Where is my tooth?" he cries.

Marge and I peer into the empty tissue.

Oh no! What a disaster. After all that, we have lost the tooth.

"Mommy always says that when you lose something, you need to think about where you had it last," I say. Marge nods in approval and we both look at Jakey.

"When did you last play with Tim?" I ask.

"I can't remember!" he groans.

"Did you bring Tim the Tooth into the bath?"

"I don't know!" Jakey sighs, and I can't remember either, so we check in the bathtub just in case, but NO TOOTH.

"Did you have Tim when we brushed our teeth?"

"I just can't think!" he exclaims.

"Maybe you swallowed Tim!" I gulp, and Jakey begins to cry.

Marge puts her ear close to Jakey's tummy.

"Interesting," she says. "I hear some fish sticks swimming around in there, and some broccoli. . . ."

"That's just what we had for dinner," I say. Can Marge really hear Jakey's food inside his tummy?

"And some apple juice," she calls out. "BUT I DO NOT hear a tooth!"

"Phew," says Jakey. But he is only relieved for a minute.

"Maybe Tim fell down the sink!" he gasps.

We all three peer into the drain. It is too dark to see anything. If Tim the Tooth is down there, he is lost forever.

"If we don't find him, the tooth fairy won't come!" wails Jakey. This is getting serious.

Marge runs downstairs and comes back
with Dad's toolbox. She digs around a bit
and pulls the wrench out again. Then she
crouches under the sink and puts the wrench
around the pipe there and we all help her
turn it round and round and round.

"Tim is probably in the first part of this piping here," Marge says. "I've seen Petunia the palace plumber do this before. You just twist and twist . . ." She chatters away.

CLUNK!

A section of the pipe falls to the floor. Inside it we find a blue marble, a wand from a bottle of bubble mixture, and a disgusting clump of hair. NO TOOTH. And now I can look down the drain and see the floor. Mommy and Dad will not like this!

"Your tooth must be farther down!" calls Marge as she begins unscrewing more pipes.

"But, Marge," I say, "isn't that where the water comes from?"

Before Marge can answer, water starts squirting out of the pipe right into her face.

"WE'VE SPRUNG A LEAK!" she shrieks.

Water is spraying all over the bathroom.

"Can anyone see Tim the Tooth? I hope he can swim," Marge calls.

"We can't see anything," Jakey and I say as water spurts everywhere. I have to think fast. I grab the tube of toothpaste and force it inside the end of the leaking pipe.

"That'll hold," says Marge in relief.

But I am not sure: the pipe is clanging and banging and quaking and shaking.

"What about my TOOTH?" yells Jakey again. "If Tim didn't go down the drain, then WHERE IS HE?"

I can tell he is about to cry when suddenly—

BRRRRING

BRRRRING!

The sound is coming from Marge's bag!

"My alarm clock! It's eight o'clock!" Marge gulps. "We have to put the LIGHTS OUT. That's what it says on your mommy's list!" Marge leaves us in the bathroom and we can hear her turning off the lights all around the house, *click, click, click.* It is getting dark, but Jakey hardly notices.

"Eight p.m. and the lights are OUT!" Marge says, taking a flashlight from Dad's toolbox. "We are following your mommy's rules PERFECTLY!"

I am not sure how destroying our bathroom fits into following Mommy's rules perfectly, but Marge is in charge.

"Now I miss my wobbly tooth." Jakey sniffles. "It was better than having a lost-forever tooth."

"Detective Marge to the rescue," Marge says seriously, while making swooping patterns with the flashlight.

"So tonight at approximately seven-thirty p.m. was the last time we saw this missing tooth?" Marge asks Jakey, shining the flashlight on his face. He nods yes.

Marge still has Mommy's list of rules. She turns it over, and together (like proper investigators) we figure out everything that we did until then. . . .

1. Made a traffic jam with toy cars

2. Ate dinner

3. Built a fort

4. Had a bath and brushed our teeth

5. DISCOVERED TIM THE TOOTH WAS MISSING!

"We have to do it all again, but backward!" declares Marge. "That's the only way we'll find Tim. Let's start with the fort."

I love building forts, and Marge is *very* good at it because of the time she helped the king build a new wing onto the palace to make room for the queen's chocolate collection.

Our rebuilt fort is even better than it was the first time around. Jakey makes wings for it out of cushions, and we fly over the kingdom in search of the missing tooth while Marge sings in her warbling voice.

"Toothy, middle bottom-left tooth,
You are in Jakey's mouth no more.

It's like you vanished with a poof.

Where you are we can't be sure."

But after all that there is still NO TOOTH.

"You played with Tim at dinner!" I remember. "We popped him into the pea bowl so he could play hide-and-seek with some friends his own size."

We race into the kitchen, and Marge swishes the apple-juice bottle (we had let Tim take a swim in there) and Jakey checks the floor (Tim the Tooth enjoyed some tobogganing on the back of an ice cube earlier), but still there is NO TOOTH.

Jakey's shoulders are beginning to sag. I haven't seen him this gloomy since he wasn't allowed to watch *The Lego Movie* because Mommy thought he was too young.

"Don't give up, Jakey. There's still the traffic jam," I say.

We arrange the cars in a long line, like we did earlier. We make the vehicles reach out of the playroom, down the stairs, and under the dining-room table. It's so much

fun because Marge doesn't believe in speed limits or keeping to one lane, and so all the cars shoot and skittle across the floor.

The whole time we make the cars shout at each other: "Hey, Lady Chittleham, have you seen a tooth?! . . . Tell your driver to slow down!"

Jakey and I make our cars honk A LOT!

In between shouts and beeps we check each car and the floor very carefully. I look inside Jakey's fast red car twice, because I remember Tim speeding over a baseball-bat bridge in it and crashing into the sofa.

But there is NO TOOTH.

By now it is getting dark, and I say a tiny prayer that if we can just find Jakey's tooth, then I will never sneak Jakey's candies from his secret box ever again.

"Right," says Marge with a sigh, "there is only one thing left to do." She reaches into Dad's toolbox and pulls out the wrench. She opens her mouth wide and puts it around one of her front teeth.

"What are you doing, Marge?" I gasp. But it's clear: she is going to pull out one of her own teeth!

"You need a tooth, Jakey," says Marge, lowering the wrench. "The tooth fairy won't care if it is yours or mine. She only pays attention to rare items like long-toothed ferrets' teeth."

"But, Marge," I say, "haven't you already lost your teeth?"

"Yes," says Marge, "I lost one in a sword fight with the grand duke of Nottingham over the last slice of lemon meringue pie. . . ."

A TOOTH FOR A MERINGUE

And I chipped one on the throne during an acrobatic performance with a one-legged duck."

Marge starts to tug.

"IT WON'T GROW BACK," shrieks Jakey in horror, but I can tell he is also a little bit excited. "You'll look like a pirate . . . or a baby . . . or a . . . WITCH!"

Marge tugs harder. She really is going to pull out her tooth! I stare at my feet. I can't look.

"Wish me luck!" Marge says, just as I remember something.

"WAIT!" I scream. "I SAW TIM THE TOOTH!"

Marge pauses as I close my eyes and try hard to picture what happened. As I was putting on my pajamas with the daisies on the pockets, I saw Jakey putting his tooth under his pillow!

I hurry to get all my words out.

"OH YES, I FORGOT!" Jakey gasps. "I put it there for the tooth fairy to collect."

My little brother is only four, so he can't be expected to remember everything. We all bolt back upstairs into our bedroom, and under Jakey's pillow we find . . .

Something small and white and just the size of a tooth!

Jakey grabs it and holds up his right arm like a champion.

"HOORAY!" He kisses the tooth.

We did it!

"You saved the day, Jemima," says Marge. But I think she is the brave one. She was going to pull out her grown-up tooth for Jakey!

Then Marge yawns. "When do the chambermaids come to tidy up?"

She always forgets that we are not royal and we do not have servants. I start to worry. What will happen when Mommy and Dad see the flooded bathroom?

The clanging, banging noise that started when I plugged up the pipe is *very* loud now. It sounds like a whale is trapped behind the bathroom wall, trying to get in.

Luckily for us, Marge has a plan. We leave Jake's tooth under his pillow with this note:

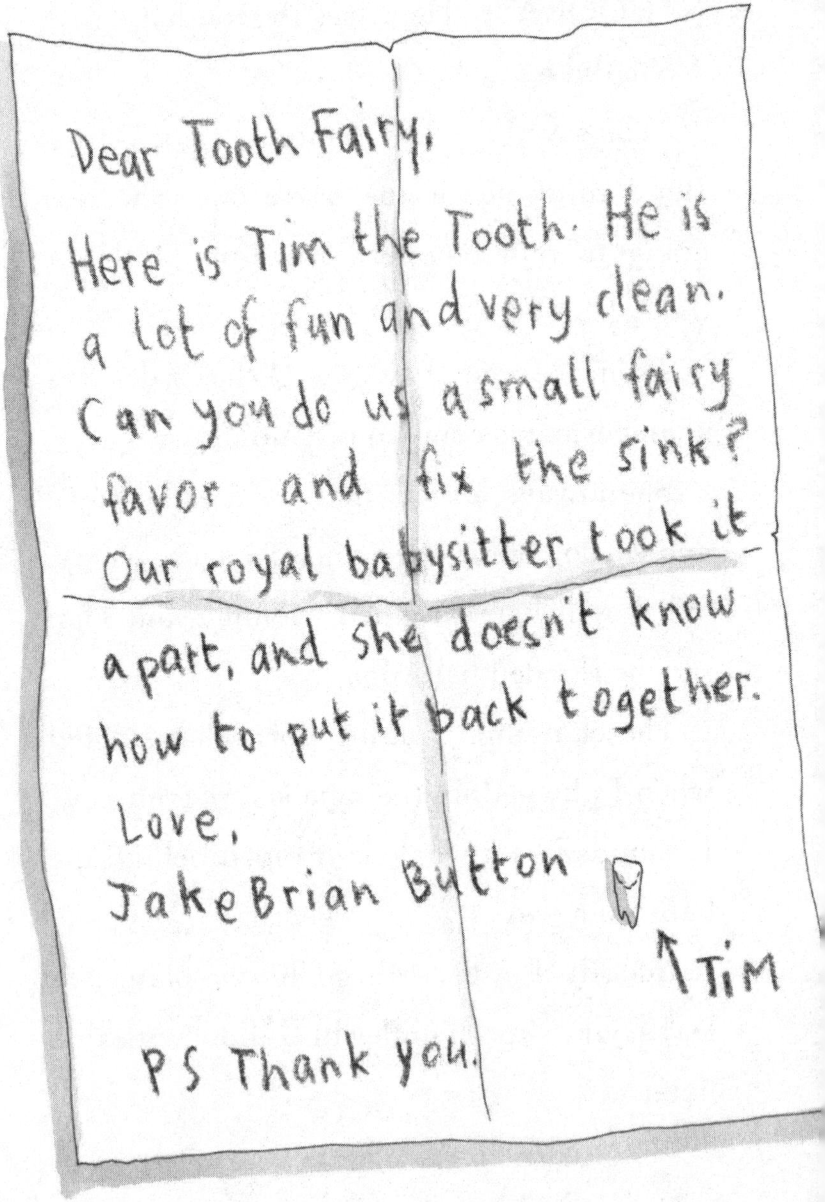

Dear Tooth Fairy,

Here is Tim the Tooth. He is a lot of fun and very clean. Can you do us a small fairy favor and fix the sink? Our royal babysitter took it apart, and she doesn't know how to put it back together.

Love,
Jake Brian Button

↑ Tim

P S Thank you.

And would you believe that when we wake up in the morning, the bathroom is spotless and there is a shiny coin under Jakey's pillow!

Marge and the Great Train Rescue

I can't believe this is actually happening to me. Two amazing things on the same day! One—Marge, the most fun grown-up on the planet, except for Mommy (and sometimes Dad), is babysitting us. Two—Mommy has arranged a visit to the zoo, and for the first time ever we are going by train.

A real *train*.

My belly is doing backflips. It's me, Jemima Button, and I am sitting on my bedroom floor while my brother plays with his toy train set. Jake has built a track that travels all the way from the kitchen into our bedroom, and I have tripped over it twice.

"Trains go faster than cars." Jakey lifts up his tank engine and whizzes it past my head.

"Planes go the fastest," I remind him.

"But trains make a cool sound," Jakey says. I kind of have to agree with him.

Jakey wants to be a train driver when he grows up. When he was little Dad used to take him to see the choo-choos, and he would always cry when it was time to come home. That's how much he loves trains.

DING DONG

That's our doorbell.

Whoopee!

Jakey and I scramble over each other as we run for the door, screaming so loudly that Mommy spills tea in her lap.

Marge is here. What a sight to see!

Marge is so small that she could be a hobbit. She even told us that once Santa Claus mistook her for an elf and asked her to help him deliver Christmas presents.

This morning Marge is wearing a long, furry pink scarf that trails all the way down her back, and a spotted pink sun hat. She looks kind of like a pink flamingo but with shorter legs.

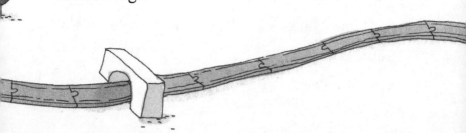

"Jolly jumbucks!" she hoots, pulling three silver train tickets out of her backpack. "We three musketeers are off on an adventure."

She takes our hands, and we all skip in a circle, shrieking.

"Hi, Marge," Mommy says, wiping brown tea off her trousers. "The train leaves at nine o'clock, and the station isn't far."

While Marge consults her pocket watch, I give Mommy a hug because I don't want her to feel left out by how pleased we are to see Marge.

"We must dash," Marge announces. "We need to be the first ones to board the train, you see. Then we can ride at the front with the admiral and look out the window at the fish when we go underwater."

"Um, Marge . . ." I giggle. "A train isn't a submarine."

"You mean, trains don't go under the sea?"
Marge squints.

Mommy laughs. Our babysitter can be so
silly.

"They do go under the sea sometimes, but
inside a *tunnel*," I explain.

Marge looks surprised but not entirely
convinced.

"Have fun on the train and enjoy the zoo,
kiddos." Mommy gives us each a brown pa-
per bag with peanut butter and jelly sandwiches inside.

"Please make sure Jakey doesn't only eat the
bread," Mommy says, and Jakey rolls his eyes.

My little brother has two rules:

1. When he is eating a sandwich,
he only eats the bread. It doesn't
matter what the filling is—he won't
eat it EVER. Even if it's jam.

2. Jakey won't stand in line. He hates being "patient" and says patience is stupid.

"And remember, kids, Marge is in charge." Mommy kisses us goodbye.

It's only once we have started the walk to the station that I notice Marge is carrying two large suitcases as well as her backpack.

ROLL ROLL

"I never leave the palace without my hat collection. It could rain or shine or we might get invited to tea and scones," Marge pants, dragging everything behind her.

I think Marge has lots of hats because she needs to hide her hair. Have I told you about Marge's hair? Our babysitter has the coolest red, green, yellow, orange, and blue hair. But she doesn't ever show it to grown-ups. Only we know her secret. I'm not sure Mommy and Dad would let Marge look after us if they saw her crazy hair or knew she has a long-toothed ferret called Burt who she trained to play the harmonica.

The train station is very busy with people scurrying this way and that. There is a big board with all the places the trains go to on it. Marge is staring at the board, and at our tickets. She looks confused.

"Platform three hundred and ninety-one," she announces after a long time.

I look over the edge of the railing and count the shiny trains and platforms beneath us. That doesn't sound right, so I take our tickets.

"That's coach three, seat number ninety-one," I say as I look carefully at the board. "We need to go to platform one."

Marge is the kind of babysitter who you sometimes have to babysit, if you get what I mean. I think it's because she grew up in a palace where she had a cook and a butler and lots of nannies to do things for her.

The platform is crammed with people, and Jakey and I hold hands because we don't want to be swept away.

TOOT TOOT

A big red train chugs down the track toward us. Jakey is grinning with all his teeth as we join the line to board.

"You broke your own rule," I tease my brother. "You are waiting in a line."

"This isn't a line. It's a squiggle." Jakey is so stubborn.

We don't get far before Marge realizes that somehow on the short ride down the escalator she has lost our tickets—or "misplaced" them, as she calls it. Luckily I am very good at finding things. Over the past year I have found Dad's reading glasses five times and Mommy's missing glove, and I even found a coin in the crack of a sidewalk.

"Look!" I spy them poking out from under her hat.

"Who put them up there? That's very odd." Marge eyes the crowd suspiciously. Jakey and I pretend to be curious, but we both know Marge must have just forgotten putting them there.

"You know, I am very handy on a train," Marge tells us. "You might say I'm an expert. When I used to ride in the queen's carriage, the king would call me Mechanical Marge." Marge is chatting as we scramble on excitedly. "This type of train is called a high-speed monorail, and it has wings so it can fly over mountains too."

"Nonsense!" says a bald man in a uniform. "A train isn't an airplane!" His name tag says HAROLD.

Jakey is staring at his head. "Who are you, and what happened to your hair?"

"I am the conductor. Now move on back, as we are leaving shortly," Harold scolds us.

The train looks much bigger on the inside. There is carpet on the floor, and all the seats are numbered, so it's not hard to find where we are supposed to be. I race to sit by the window. Jakey sits next to me, and once Marge has heaved her suitcases onto the shelf above us, she sits opposite. Every time I think about how fast the train will go, my tummy feels kind of weird and tingly.

"The royal train has a special carriage for pet grooming. I used to take my albino water buffalo to have his tail washed and—" Marge begins.

Before she can finish her sentence, a voice

booms over the loudspeaker.

"Attention, passengers, the train is about to depart. Please stand clear of the closing doors."

There is a gentle HUM as the train slides out of the station and gathers speed.

"Look!" Jakey points out the window at

the trees and buildings whizzing past. "We are going so fast."

We *are* going way faster than when I ride my bike and a lot faster than the tallest slide at school. I am definitely feeling nervous until Marge begins to sing in her warbly voice.

"It doesn't fly in the air
or swim through the sea.
It's longer than a car
and slower than a star.
It keeps you dry in the rain.
It's not a coat. . . . It's a train."

Again a voice comes over the loudspeaker:

"Good afternoon. My name is Gerard, and I am your engineer for the day. We expect no delays."

"Please can I drive the train?" Jakey begs.

"Of course." Marge pats his head.

You know how grown-ups always say that something is going to happen and it doesn't? Like when Dad says he will water Mommy's plants or Mommy says that we can go on the fun ride outside the supermarket? Marge never does that. If Marge says Jakey will drive the train, he will. I am just not sure how safe that will be for the other passengers.

"Come on, then—let's find Gerard, the engineer." Marge stands up, and we make our way through the cars toward the front of the train.

Trying to walk on a moving train is a little like trying to stand up on a swing.

We keep losing our balance and having to grab onto things. At one point, I fall on top of a lady who is sleeping in her seat. Thankfully she doesn't wake up, but Jakey gets the giggles.

Finally we reach the glass doors that lead to where the driver sits. Marge is about to slide them open when we hear a stern voice.

"Stop in the name of railroad safety!"

We turn to see Harold again.

"Exactly what do you think you are doing?" he demands.

Marge curtsies.

"My name is Margery Beauregard Victoria Ponterfois, and I am a duchess. We have a request for the driver."

"NO ONE except the driver is allowed inside the driver's cab. Not even a duchess," Harold states.

"But how can Jakey drive the train from *outside* the driver's cab?" Marge asks.

Harold's face is a little bit like a balloon that's having too much air pushed into it.

"Drive the train?" His face is going from red to purple. "This child doesn't even have a license! Have you lost your marbles?!"

"No, but I did lose our train tickets for a moment. Thankfully, Jemima found them inside my hat." Marge smiles.

Harold's eyebrows look like they are sliding off his face in fury. "Passengers never drive the train!!"

"Jakey has had a lot of practice driving his toy trains actually, so there's no need to be afraid," Marge replies.

"I am not afraid of anything!" Harold sniffs.

"Not of the dark or spiders or even loud thunder. And I'm definitely not afraid of three small children!" He marches us back to our seats.

"But I'm a grown-up," Marge corrects him.

"Then you should know better. A child? Driving a train? What's next, a monkey flying a spacecraft?!"

"Actually, the first animal in space was a monkey named Albert," Marge tells him.

"Nonsense!" Harold stomps off.

We all slide glumly into our seats. I can see Jakey's eyes are filling with water.

I feel sad too. For a moment I thought that Jakey was going to get to drive the train. It would have made him so happy and been such a wonderful story to tell our friends.

But Marge already has a plan. We are going to wear disguises! Marge calls this "going undercover," and it means we can sneak our way back to the driver's cab without Harold catching us.

Our babysitter's eyes twinkle as she pulls down her suitcases.

Marge finds a blue fedora for Jakey. "Your spy name is Jake Bond." She plonks a navy-blue beret (which is a fancy hat that French people wear) on my head. "Your spy name is Sneaky Baguette."

Finally she finds a furry cap for herself. "And I shall be known as Stealthy Squirrel."

Next she finds sunglasses for us all.

"Harold will still see that it is us," I say worriedly.

But no one listens to me. "Marge is in charge!" Jakey grins.

Just as we are about to set off on the mission, Marge remembers something.

"We need to wear gloves," she says,

hunting through her suitcase, "so we don't leave any fingerprints."

It turns out Marge doesn't have any gloves, so she suggests we wear socks on our hands instead. It feels a bit strange (and itchy) wearing sock mittens. Marge decides that we may have to split up if we are spotted. "I don't want to split up!" Jakey looks scared for a second. "That bald man is very strict."

Because he is so brave, it's easy to forget that my little brother is only four years old.

"Don't worry, Jake Bond. Sneaky Baguette and Stealthy Squirrel will stay with you!" I say, giving him a hug.

We move swiftly through the car, trying to not make eye contact with anyone or lose our balance. My beret keeps slipping over one eye and we are getting strange looks from people. Jakey's polka-dot "gloves" are too big and come up to his elbows. He looks half boy, half dalmatian puppy.

Just as we are almost at the front of the train, we spy Harold collecting tickets.

"Hide!" Jakey yelps as he pulls us into the bathroom and locks the door.

This room is too small for three people.

We are all squashed together like toes in a slipper. Above the sound of the engine we can hear footsteps and chatter.

Jakey slides the door open and takes a peek. "The coast is clear!"

We make a dash for it, huffing and puffing up the last bit of the car. We are about to go into the driver's cab when

SCREEEEEECCHHHH!!!

There is a piercing sound followed by the hiss of the brakes, and we tumble forward as the train grinds to a STOP.

Gerard's voice comes over the loudspeaker again. "Sorry for the delay. It appears that we have a problem on the tracks."

"I'm never going to drive the train now that it's broken!" Jakey pouts.

"Mechanical Marge to the rescue," Marge cries.

We peer out of the window, looking for a clue. All I can see are trees and a water tower and a car on a faraway road. Jakey runs to the other side of the train to get a different view. I hope that we are not stuck for too long.

"I think the twin engine and the hover blades have sprung a leak," Marge concludes.

"LOOK!" I say. There, standing on the tracks and looking very relaxed, is a big brown . . . COW!

Harold is pacing up and down and doesn't seem to have noticed that we have sneaked our way back *or* that we are wearing silly hats.

He faces us and all the passengers. "As you can see, there is a wild and vicious beast blocking our path, and only when it moves on can we continue with our journey."

Wild and vicious? I am confused. I stare more closely. There is green grass all over the tracks, and the cow is chomping happily. "That cow might never move on," I say. "The zoo will be closed by the time we get there."

"We'll just have to wait," Harold warns. "It's not safe for anyone to go out there. That

monster could tear our limbs from our bodies. It could eat us alive and trample our bones!"

I shake my head. Poor Harold must be scared of cows.

"I've never heard of a killer cow," Jakey whispers to Marge.

"I have," Marge whispers back. "But that's another story."

Then she looks at Harold. "I thought you weren't afraid of anything," she reminds him.

"I thought so too . . . until I saw that hairy, scary monster cow!" He starts to sob.

Marge places a socked hand on Harold's shoulder. "Would you like us to help?" she asks. "I am incredibly fond of cattle. I once dressed up my pet cow Annabella as a

Learning to pirouette: grace embodied. ♥

ballerina and taught her to pirouette."

Harold nods in relief. "Yes, please."

And that's how Jakey, Marge, and I find ourselves on the edge of the tracks, just a few minutes later, heading toward the cow.

Marge makes a weird clicking sound with her tongue and claps her hands. The cow stares at us as Marge rummages inside her backpack and pulls out our peanut butter and jelly sandwiches.

Oh no. Mommy won't like this one bit. Marge is giving our lunch away to stray animals!

"*Yassou* is Greek for 'hello,' and as I suspected, this is a Greek cow," Marge tells us as she stops and gets down on all fours and MOOs at the cow.

The cow's ears flick backward and forward like the windshield wipers on a car.

Slowly she starts walking toward Marge and then turns to me.

Oh my goodness. Why has this cow picked me? I don't speak Greek. Marge passes me a sandwich and I hold it out to the cow, who is getting closer and closer. She has round curious eyes fringed with long eyelashes. My hand starts to shake a little as the cow lowers her head. I can feel hot breath and whiskers tickling my palm as she takes the sandwich inside her lips. She chews for a moment and then spits out some peanut butter.

"I told you, Jemima," Jakey whispers, being careful not to startle her. "Even cows like only the bread!"

I can't believe it! I am feeding a cow. I let my palm touch the velvety fur on her nose. It's so soft.

Marge looks on proudly. Then she stands up and makes the clicking sound again. And would you believe that the cow starts following her? Marge, Jakey, and I lead the animal off the tracks and over to where the rest of the herd is standing by the trees.

I am puffed up with pride as I high-five Jakey and Marge. We did it!

When we're back aboard, the rest of the passengers give us three cheers.

Harold looks very relieved. "Would you like to come and meet the driver?" he offers.

Jakey is so thrilled that he blows an underarm raspberry. He only does this when something is incredibly exciting, like the time he found the face paints after Mommy had hidden them.

Gerard, the driver, has a bushy mustache and seems delighted to have visitors. Particularly ones who have helped him keep his train on schedule.

He shakes our hands. "You must be the Cattle Herders who saved the day. Welcome!"

Jakey and I can't believe how many buttons there are in the driver's cab. Gerard shows us the brake and throttle controls. We see a big blue computer screen with control-indicator

lights and another panel that reads FUEL
SYSTEM. Jakey pulls the horn.

TOOT TOOT

It must all be too much for Marge, because
while Gerard is explaining what everything
does, she gives a big yawn.

"You know, Greek cows are very friendly
by nature—not like Spanish cows," Marge
murmurs as she curls up in the corner. Her

furry cap is still on, and her little legs are poking out as she promptly falls fast asleep.

Now, what happens next is the most amazing thing ever, even more amazing than all the incredible animals that we will get to see later. . . .

Finally, Jakey is allowed to hold the throttle!

I get a lump in my throat as I watch. His little tongue is poking out in concentration, and he looks so proud of himself! I can't wait to tell Dad that Jakey drove the train.

Then, can you believe it, I get a turn too.

I can't do a somersault yet or snap my fingers . . . but I, Jemima Button, the Cattle Herder, can drive a train!

Marge and the Zany Zoo Day

It's me again, Jemima Button, and I have great news—we made it to the zoo!

On our long walk from the train station Marge sang a silly song that gave Jakey and me the giggles.

"There's no place like the zoo.
You can ride on a kangaroo.
You can feed a crocodile too.
Just don't step in animal poo."

We have had such a fantastic day already, and now we get to see all our favorite animals!

"I can't wait to see Oliver the Orangutan!"

My little brother is jumping over the cracks in the sidewalk.

Oliver the Orangutan is the reason Jakey loves the zoo. He's so big and furry, and he sort of acts like a human. He and Jakey are best zoo friends: last time we came here, they

had a dance-off. Whatever my brother did, the orangutan would copy him. Even the zookeeper was laughing. But when Jakey took a turn at following Oliver, it all went wrong.

The orangutan turned his bottom to everyone and started flinging his poop at

the glass. That's when Mommy decided it was time to leave. We haven't been back to the zoo since, until today!

We join the line of people at the entrance. I don't even mind waiting to get inside because I am so excited. Marge has let me look after the money for our tickets. I feel like such a big girl!

Did I tell you that I am doing a project in school on chameleons? They are a kind of lizard that can change color. I have brought all my colored pencils (because I don't know which color the chameleon will be today), and I am going to sketch one.

The line is moving very slowly. "Look—I can see the giraffes from here!" I point at where two giraffes are looking over the zoo fence and chewing slowly, their long purple tongues slipping out to catch stray grass.

Jakey and I watch them for a minute before I realize things have gone strangely quiet.

We turn back, and Marge is nowhere to be seen.

"MARGE?!" I call out.

"MARGE?!" Jakey repeats.

But there is no answer. Where has she gone? We walk through the line shouting loudly.

"MARGE! HERE, MARGE!" says Jakey.

"Have you lost your dog?" asks one lady very kindly.

"No," I tell her, "we've lost our babysitter."

"Have you seen her?" Jakey asks. "She's about this tall"—he holds his hand up to my forehead—"and she has rainbow hair and she looks like an Oompa-Loompa from *Charlie and the Chocolate Factory*."

The lady looks at us strangely, but just

then I spy Marge way up ahead of us. She's wearing sunglasses and crawling along the ground toward the ticket gates!

"Excuse me," I cry as Jakey and I race to the front of the line. Ahead of us, Marge crawls between the legs of the man selling tickets, slides past the gates, and ducks behind a bush. She's inside the zoo, and no one is stopping her!

We try to follow, but the man at the gate
stops us.

"Is there a grown-up with you?" he asks.
"Children can't enter the zoo alone."

'Um, yes ... she went, er, ahead of us,' I
stammer.

He doesn't look as if he believes me, so I hand over the money that Marge gave us.

He studies us for a minute, tips his zoo-worker hat, and waves us through. He even gives us free tokens for animal food.

Phew, we are in!

Marge pops out from behind a bush.

"Marge, you didn't pay for a ticket!" I scold her.

"I have a pass for the full year," Marge says, slipping her shades off. She shows it to us proudly.

"Then why did you sneak in?" I ask.

"I'm not technically allowed back in the zoo after the last time," Marge confesses in a whisper.

"What happened the last time?" Jakey's eyes are as round as golf balls.

I am not quite sure I want to know the

answer. Whatever it is, Mommy probably wouldn't like it.

"Last time I was here," Marge admits, "I accidentally opened some cages and set a few of the animals free. I released Grace the Warthog—she looked so glum! Then I freed Sam the Lion, or as I named him, Sad-Sam-Stuck-in-His-Cage." Marge looks embarrassed. "But freedom has its price.

All the zoo visitors were screaming!

"Then the zookeepers organized a big search. Eventually we found Sam and Grace.

Sam was snoozing in the butterfly house.

Grace was in the cafeteria, helping herself to hot dogs.

"So it was all absolutely hunky-dory, but the head zookeeper told me that I'd better not come back."

Jakey looks as happy as can be. "Let's let Oliver the Orangutan free so he can come home with us!" he begs.

That is the worst idea ever! I share a bedroom with Jake, and it already looks like a giant mess *before* an orangutan moves in.

We open up a map of the zoo. "Well, young explorers," says Marge, "where shall we go first?"

"Let's see Oliver the Orangutan," Jakey cries.

"I think we should see the baby tigers first," I suggest. Oliver is all the way at the bottom of the map, and there are amazing animals nearby that can't be missed. Marge agrees, and off we go. I feel like skipping, so I do. Marge and Jakey join in, and we decide that's how we will get around the zoo.

The tiger enclosure is massive, and it takes us a while to spot the babies. There are two of them, and a sign tells us that the cubs are now six months old.

"That's about your age in tiger years, Jemima," says Marge, watching them. "You know, I spent some time traveling with the circus years ago. They called me a tiger whisperer, because I speak tiger. And I'm very good at whispering."

Marge shows us how to whisper to the tigers, but the cubs are busy playing together, chasing a rubber ball. They don't seem to be very good at listening. Maybe we are not whispering about the right things. I try to think of interesting secrets to tell the baby tigers. Like that I used to believe that stuffed animals came alive when I went to sleep, or that getting new shoes made you run faster.

Our whispering gets louder and louder, and everyone at the tiger enclosure is staring at us *except* for the tigers. Then Marge starts hissing and growling at them! Now the cubs pay attention. They both freeze, whimper, and dart into their little cave.

Marge has scared them away! The zookeeper looks angry as he heads toward us.

"Let's move along," says Marge in one last whisper.

We have barely continued our journey before my brother pipes up again.

"Now can we see Oliver the Orangutan?"

I tell him that we have a few other animals to see first and he has to learn patience. We say hi to the elephants and spy on the hippos having a bath. We wave at the zebras and show the flamingos how we can stand on one leg too.

When we arrive at the penguin habitat, we sit in a small crowd and watch a zookeeper throwing slimy fish to the penguins.

"Who wants to feed them some mackerel?" the zookeeper asks. All the children put their hands up, but Marge is the only adult who does.

"Ooooh, ooooh, pick me please, me, me!" Marge shouts.

"Are you a child or a grown-up?" the zookeeper asks.

"A grown-up! Please pick her," Jakey says, jumping up and down.

The zookeeper hands Marge the bucket of fish. Marge picks up an extra-slimy one and holds it in the air. The penguins are flapping around excitedly.

Then Marge holds the fish up even higher above her head, opens her mouth, and drops the slippery fish straight in! I don't know who gasps louder, the people or the penguins.

"Ah, I love mackerel," says Marge. "So good for you too. All those healthy fish oils."

The penguins and the people stare at her.

"Jakey, Jemima—fancy a treat?"

I shake my head firmly. A wet fish is not a treat—YUCK!

To everyone's horror, Marge gulps down a few more fish. Then she carefully places two in her backpack for later and feeds the rest to the penguins, who still look a little annoyed with her.

"After that delicious lunch," she tells Jake and me as we leave the penguin habitat, "it's time for ice cream!"

While I am having a strawberry Creamsicle and Jakey is eating four scoops of mint chocolate chip, I look at the map again.

We're very close to the petting zoo, which is one of the most fun things to do. Jakey and I use our tokens to buy food. Now that we are experienced Cattle Herders, we feel very sure of ourselves around the cows, ducks, sheep, and goats.

Marge perches on a rock in the middle of the enclosure, and all the animals surround us.

Jakey and I feed them and pet them. One of the cows is brown all over, and I can't help wishing she could make chocolate milk instead of regular.

She keeps rubbing her head on my back. I want to show Marge, but she has her hands full.

She is holding a goat in her arms like a baby, covering it with kisses while singing a lullaby!

Then she kisses a duck, right on its beak. She does the same with all the sheep too, even the ones that run away. She just chases them down until she catches them and lays a giant smooch on their dusty, dirty sheep noses. Marge loves animals more than anyone I know!

As we are leaving the petting zoo, the keeper shows us where to wash our hands.

"You might want to wash your mouth, too," he advises Marge.

"*Now* can we go to Oliver the Orangutan?" asks Jakey, hopping from foot to foot. "I've waited *ages*."

"Soon, Jakey," I tell him. I have found the reptile and insect house on the map, where I am pretty sure the chameleon lives. I point it out to Marge, and we all skip off.

It's dark and damp in the reptile and insect

house, and I have to blink a few times to see the displays. Jakey takes my hand, and we walk over to the first glass enclosure.

Right away Marge spots Katie the Chameleon. She's bright green and scaly and clinging to a rock.

I take out my pencils to start drawing her. She's so still and doesn't move an inch. I wait for a more dramatic pose.

Jakey starts getting fidgety and moves on.

"Look in this window!" He gulps.

I race over to where he is.

It's dark, but lit with a small orange light. There are some branches and rocks inside and a . . . furry-legged, big-headed tarantula spider!

"ARRGHH!" Marge shrieks. "HELP! SPIDER!"

She jumps onto my back and clings on like superglue.

"We are in the insect house—of course there are spiders!" I say. "Although actually, spiders are not insects. They are arachnids." But Marge doesn't seem to be listening, and everyone is staring at us. I am giving a grown-up a piggyback!

"It's going to attack me!" Marge continues. She is surprisingly not very heavy for a grown-up.

"It's behind the glass!" I try to calm her.

"Surely it could smash the glass with its pointy poisonous fangs!" Marge panics.

"That one isn't even venomous," I say, moving closer to read what's written about

it, forgetting Marge is now closer to the spider too.

"ARRGGHH!" Marge screams as loudly as she can. Then, as if the whole building is on fire, she leaps off my back and jumps over a baby in his stroller, landing on the floor with a bump. Still terrified, she springs up and dives through a whole class of school-children, pushing their teacher aside and el-bowing a grandfather on her way out.

When Jakey and I find her, she is still trembling in fear.

"When I lived in the palace, the king had every one of those beastly creepy-crawlies captured and banished to another kingdom."

I am so surprised. I always imagined that Marge loved all creatures, even slugs.

"But we have to go back inside. I need to

finish my drawing," I say.

Before Marge can answer, a voice booms over the loudspeaker.

"Come one, come all to the
Aviary Show,
happening right now
in Parrot Cove!"

Marge claps her hands gleefully.

"I *love* parrots. I had one once called Lady Biscuit, but she fell in love with a badger and eloped."

"When are we going to see Oliver the Orangutan?" Jakey whines.

"Next, I promise," I tell my little brother. "I still have to finish my school project."

We check the zoo map

and skip our way to Parrot Cove. We take a seat in the front. Birds the color of Marge's hair are swooshing through the air back and forth. They are so beautiful!

A hawk flaps past, collects a ring, and returns it.

SOAR

A parrot chatters away.
A rainbow lorikeet
sails over our heads.
We all cheer.

SQUAWK

SWOOP

Once the show is over, Marge removes a bag of seed from her backpack and pours it into a little pile on her hat.

"Stay quiet and don't move," she tells us, and sure enough, all the birds start flying around, and some of them are landing on Marge's head and snacking. It's wonderful to see them so close, particularly the snowy owl, who looks like a little old man with reading glasses on.

"Now can we go to Oliver the Orangutan?" Jakey nags.

"Now can we go to Oliver the Orangutan?" a red parrot repeats.

"Now can we go to Oliver the Orangutan?" squawks another yellow parrot.

Soon a green one chimes in and then a blue and they are all chorusing:

"NOW CAN WE GO TO OLIVER THE ORANGUTAN?"

It is *really* starting to annoy me. I feel like it's the only sentence I have heard all day. I am just about to tell Jakey off when I see something white and sticky whizzing by me. It lands on Marge's hat!

It takes me a second to realize what is happening as another dollop falls down and lands with a PLOP on my shoulder. *Oh no!* The birds are pooping. Another load drops with a SPLAT on Jakey's head.

"EWWW, RUN!" I yell.

"Getting pooped on is good luck!" Marge puffs as we make a dash to the bathroom. "Chester my meerkat once pooped on my foot during a game of hide-and-seek, and sure enough, I was never found!"

A BLESSING IN DISGUISE.

We clean ourselves up with wet wipes, and then at last we skip off to see Oliver the Orangutan. Even though he is driving me crazy, I know how much my little brother has been looking forward to this, so I don't want anything to spoil it.

But would you believe what happens next? As we get close, we notice that the whole area where Oliver lives is empty!

He's not on the rope swing, he's not lying on his netting hammock, and he is not up his favorite tree. Poor Jakey starts to panic.

I suddenly see a big sign and read it aloud.

OLIVER IS VISITING THE VET.
HE WILL BE BACK NEXT WEDNESDAY.

Jakey's face is crumpling. My little brother has two rules:

1. He always wears his boots in summer and sandals in the winter.

2. He only goes to the zoo to see Oliver the Orangutan.

Jakey's shoulders sag and his bottom lip is wobbling. I feel so bad for him. He is starting to cry, and I can tell he is going to howl. A whole class of children has arrived and seems just as disappointed.

"I want to see Oliver," wails a girl in pigtails.

I give my little brother a huge hug, but then I realize that Marge is missing again. I can't believe that Mommy told Marge to keep an eye on us, but we're the ones who should be keeping an eye on Marge!

"Ohh aahhh oooh ahhh!"

We turn in surprise. A grunting sound is coming from the corner of the cage. Then we see some rustling in a bush inside Oliver's enclosure.

"Look," the teacher announces to her group of schoolchildren. "What's that?"

"Oliver must be back from the vet!" I feel so relieved as I grin at Jakey.

But it's *Marge* who pops her head out of the bush!

She is wearing an orange hat and thumping her chest. To be honest, she looks more like a traffic cone than an orangutan, but no one seems to mind.

Marge swings from
rope to rope,

then she shrieks as
she grooms herself,

before she runs
to the glass and
beats it exactly
like Oliver does.

There is such a commotion that the zookeeper comes to investigate. He looks extremely angry, but just then a bigger crowd of children starts to appear. They are clapping and cheering, and no one minds at all that it isn't the real Oliver.

Jakey shuffles forward and starts playing with Marge like he usually does with Oliver.

He shakes his head "no" and Marge copies him. Then he starts laughing and Marge mimics him too.

Marge is even better than Oliver at being an orangutan.

Jakey is happy and so am I—but I haven't even told you the best part yet.

After Marge's show, the zookeeper lets me meet Katie the Chameleon up close.

She has a long curly tail, and when Marge puts her on top of her head, she turns all the colors of the rainbow. I finally get to sketch her, and I use every single one of my colored pencils!

Jakey and I look at each other and share a secret smile. We truly have the best baby-sitter in the world!

ISLA FISHER

has worked in TV and film for twenty-five years. She has played many fun and varied characters, but her favorite role is being a mom to her three children. Isla has been making up stories at bedtime for them every night since they were born, which is how *Marge in Charge* began.